“FROM MY HEART TO YOURS”

MANYA JAIN

TO MY PARENTS

Contents

About The Author

Manya Jain is currently a student at Spring Dale Senior School, Amritsar. She has a passion for writing and jointing down her feelings in form of words. She also loves to record her daily life through a journal. She also loves to put her emotions out in form of dance and drawing. This shall be her first book. She loves listening to music and spending quality time with her loved ones. She believes if you really want something and work hard enough for it, no one in the world can stop you to achieve your goal. Always remember to believe in yourself, no matter what anyone says. Just do it.

If you can imagine it, you can achieve it. If you can dream it, you can become it. -William Arthur Ward-

Preface

This book contains a set of poems with have been written with utmost love. Sometimes you just stop feeling things because you are tired of getting hurt each time you allow yourself to feel. So you just want to flip the switch of emotions off so that nothing could break you. There are times in my life when I watched every step I took as I was afraid. I was scared. These poems reflect my true self to the readers and tell them who am I as an individual and what experiences have led to me to be who I am.

I thank my parents, who are always there whenever I need them.

My friends, who always encouraged me and correct me on my mistakes.

Tanmay and Saanvi, who beard with me at night when I was working on something.

Manasvi, who inspired me.

Last but not least, to my readers for choosing my book to read. I appreciate all the love and support I get

Preface

This book contains a set of poems with have been written with utmost love. Sometimes you just stop feeling things because you are tired of getting hurt each time you allow yourself to feel. So you just want to flip the switch of emotions off so that nothing could break you. There are times in my life when I watched every step I took. I was afraid. I [illegible]. These poems [illegible] to the readers and tell them who am I as an individual [illegible] experiences have led to me [illegible] who I am.

I thank my parents, who are always there whenever I need them.

My friends, who always encouraged me and correct me on my mistakes.

[illegible] who [illegible] hand [illegible] working on [illegible].

[illegible], who inspired me.

Last but not least [illegible]

I appreciate all the love and support I get.

Acknowledgements

I would like to thank all the people who have been there to support and help me all the time. Especially my parents, my friends, my siblings, and my teachers. I would like this opportunity to tell you all that this is the outcome of your love and support. I would have been nowhere without you. I would especially like to thank my friends who encouraged me and made me believe that I can do this. I am extremely grateful to my parents. It would not be possible without them. I also want to thank Manasvi, my sister, my inspiration.

I shall also like to thank Notion Press for trusting me. I am very thankful for the support that you have provided me. I apologize if I miss someone out but you know this is your support and encouragement that has given me the confidence to write as well as create this.

Lastly, I would like to thank you readers for choosing this book. I hope you enjoy reading it.

1. Hide and seek

I have been playing the game of hide and seek from love
since I was just a little girl
I want to be chased
but not to be found
I want to hide in dark
but I am afraid to get lost in my heart
Now I longer wish to play this game
I want to be found
I want to be saved
but I am just afraid to let you know me by
who I really am
will you love me
or
just leave me like everybody else ?

2. Voice in my head

When people think I'm absent and think I don't care
I'm usually inside my head with the thoughts I cannot share
these voices aren't unstopping
they keep me awake at night
they laugh at me when I look in the mirror
even hard and when I cry
it opens its cruel mouth every day
and says " you are not good enough"
sometimes I just feel to give up
it makes me ignore every compliment I get
"they are lying" it adds in the end
these voices aren't stopping
they are haunting me to hell
sometimes I just wonder how do these
voices end up in my head

3. Fantasy girls

I'm not the girl who is loved by all
I don't like to wear heels or go to balls
I don't dream of wearing a diamond ring
nor I can sing
I've watched Disney movies 100 times
they promised us a tall dark and handsome boys
but I know there's something else waiting for me
my hopes and dreams have a fairy tale ending just for me
I know I'm perfect in my own way
no matter what world thinks of me
I don't need a Prince Charming
I'm queen of my own
I guess I'm just different from other
fantasy girls

4. Why do I have to keep pretending?

Everyone knows me as an Angel
but I'm not a stranger to a devil
hiding bullets beneath my skin
pretending to be strong as everybody else
scared to show my broken self
scared to be crushed by my loved ones
a voice passing through my head
"no one loves you as you are "
I'm brave
I'm bruised
I'm what I was meant to be
I'm a bright light locked in a dark room
why can't you see it?
I'm a warrior fighting against all my odds
this is me
why do I have to hide the real me?
why don't I deserve to be loved?
Does life have to be so rough?
why I'm scared to be seen?
Why do I have to make apologies?
why I can't talk to anyone about how I really feel?
why do I have to cry silently?

to survive in this cold-hearted world
why do I have to keep pretending?

5. Mysterious starry night

Every night I lay on the ground
looking up into the sky
wondering how the stars shine every night
doesn't it get tired of people's expectations?
doesn't want to give up
and be really who it is?
maybe it's hiding something
deep down its bright light
scared to show the world
every scar of its suffering life
or maybe it's just in my head
who knows the mysterious life of
mysterious starry night

6. Peer Pressure

Sometimes in life, it's hard to tell
what I should do and what not to do
just because my friends are doing something
should I do it too
I want so much to be appreciated
I want so bad to fit in
should I follow the crowd
or that's just a crime?
everyone tells me what should be done with my life
but what about my expectations for my own life
should I listen to my heart or my mind
should I listen to everyone or the voice coming from inside
stop laughing at me
it's much pressure on me
I'm just 15
give me some time
stop asking me questions about my life
I have high goals and a large will
but all this pressure is pressing me down
please stop I can explode any second now

7. Self Love

I want to be loved
like the moon loves the sun
I want to be held tightly by someone
who feels that I am worthy of something
I want to be adored
like when the clouds watch the birds as they soar
I want to be saved as dew dropped
when they are bubbled
on top of daffodil leaves
sleeping under the palm tree
I want to feel complete
like when you were a child
and wet grass tickle your bare feet
there's blood on your knees
but you pay no attention
because you know that you're
safe in your mother's arms
Oh no
I know how this one goes
I am walking down a road that has no end
I am reading the signs that say
please turn around
my friend

but the thing is
it's too late for me now
so I will crawl on my hands and knees
use the last bit of energy left in me
To find the love
that's already in me I learned to love myself before anyone else
I will be the moon to my sun
until my time on this road is done
I will love myself

8. If I was a book

if I was a book
do you think you would read all the pages?
do you think you would come back and take notes?
Would you love me at all my stages?
Would you judge me by my first draft?
Would you ask about the ribbed chapters
or the drops from the tear shed?
would you want to rewrite me
change all the words somehow
or remove some characters
or maybe even add some back in now?
would you judge me by my cover?
the one God carefully drew
would you fall in love with me
the same way
I fell in love with you

9. Who am I?

I met a girl who is like
the first night of summer
when everything feels limitless and warm
she is like reading your favourite book
when you can only hear the sound of the storm
she is like a warm cup of hot chocolate
maybe a shot of tequila or three
like everything is right in the world
a place only with the prettiest view
she is like hearing a good song
and needing to play it infinite times
she is like a long sappy love poem
but the one with only
thoughtful rhymes
but deep inside she feels
that there is something empty
like something is breaking inside her
which feels like hell
every time she looks at her reflection in the mirror
she can see her inner soul screaming at her
like her inner demons are taking over her soul
killing sweet lovable person everyone thinks she is
who is she really know

an angel or demon
fighting through everything
just to know a question
who am I?

10. Villain's tale

I always wonder why I liked villains more
and I think it's because when they get on the floor
down on their knees
sacrificing all his needs
just to be with
her and only her
something happens inside me
a hero would sacrifice the world
to show their love is indeed pure-hearted and honest
he would fight with anyone for her
but a villain would tear the world apart
if she was hurt
he would fight with anyone to keep her safe, now
that's a promise
they seem selfish manipulative and rude to everyone around
but he treats her like a queen
his only his
sitting beside them on the throne
with her crown
ruling the kingdom by his side
I think villains are misjudged
we don't get to know their side of the story
and maybe if we knew the hero might no longer be seen

as full of glory
monsters are made not born
any soul broken
abused and tortured would not have time to mourn
so next time I defend a villain's tale
remember they were also once broken and frail

11. Waiting at your doorstep

I guess I am not worried
because I know love will find me
when the time is right
if love was a house
I am already standing at its doorstep
waiting for it to open its door
when the time is right and
it opens its door I will be standing right there
ready to walk in
ready to be with you for my entire life
ready to give my heart to someone
who will give me his
until then I will be
waiting at your doorstep
ringing the doorbell

12. Second chances

Red flags became green lights
lighting fire in the gas station
you modified into the person I hate
from the person I once admired
you want me in the first place, right?
then what happened
what changed you
I have a hard time trusting people
but I can't blame only you for that
even after what all you did
I gave you a million chances
but you choose to break them
I guess I have a problem
of giving people second chances
I should have seen this coming
this cycle goes on and on
if my life would be a book
his chapter would be named as
"unconscious consequences"

13. Is love ugly?

The broken heart always heals
but it leaves its scar to remain
at this point, I have memorized all
parts that will never be the same
I am afraid to laugh loudly
I am scared that love doesn't know how to stay
worried that anxiety stays forever
wondering if I was born this way
I wish I didn't know this feeling
people wondering how you break
waiting for someone to love me
when they say they already did
because action says so much more than words
I wish I didn't know the feeling
waiting for someone to come back
for them to forget you all over again
ya, that night I heard my heart break
if love is so beautiful
why does it make me feel so ugly?

14. What is a friend?

Someone once asked me, “ what is a friend?”
a Stumbled for a sec
and then said
a friend is like a four leave clover
hard to find and
lucky to have
it’s like your other half
who knows you more than yourself
it’s like a magic wand
who knows the solution to your every problem
even if they don’t know the solution to their own problems
it’s like a shield
which protects you from your inside and outside demons
it is the only person you need to survive in this cruel world
it’s like your shadow
always there when you need someone to talk
it is the only person who will listen
and understand you as you are
they are like stars
you can’t see them all time
but you know they will be always by your side
they will do anything to make you laugh
even if they have to slice someone into half

I am so grateful to have a friend in my life
they are not my heart
they are my whole life

15. Being a teenager is not easy

Everyone thinks being a teenager is easy
but the reality is hidden behind the perfect smiley faces
taking alone time doesn't mean
we only care for phones
maybe because we know it can't harm us
feeling a test doesn't mean
it's the fault of our friends
maybe we didn't understand the syllabus
getting a bad grade doesn't mean
we didn't try our best maybe
we are handling so much stress
they think we make stupid mistakes
because we love too
they think we lash out because
we like to
but that is sometimes what we really need to do
the whole outside world pressurize us
and our parents we don't need them to judge us
They tell us "we also went through the same thing"
but there was a different world when you are kids
there were rainbows and children running here and there happily

but it's 2022
time has changed
we have changed understand that
because being a teenager is not easy

16. Teenager feelings

Teenager Feelings are changing me
it's making me love the sky
sweet feelings complete my day
taking my breath away
dancing alone.........singing on a microphone
it is showing me the real face of the world
which is not as pretty as I thought
I spend wonderful days
with nights looking at the moon
these feelings are taking control
I am losing with the simple little girl I was
crazy things go by....
it will to
I guess this is just the beginning of a new chapter in my life
I do careless and nonsense things
smiling and dreaming wonderful things
I guess
Teenager Feelings are changing me

17. To love of my life

To love of my life,
I miss you
there has not a day passed
when I didn't think of you
every time I look at the moon
I can see your face
why did you leave me alone at this cruel place?
you promise me that we will get through it together
but now I am just sitting here alone
staying at your photo
I miss how you use to wake me up every day
sometimes I can still see your face
I miss how you use to tie my shoelace
even when I was 11
I miss how you use to drive me to school every day
and say "Hey enjoy your day it will be better than yesterday "
why god took you away from me?
how will I survive without you telling me
it will be okay
I can't survive without you being at my side
I miss you
but remember you always be alive in my heart
no matter what happens

I love you dadu

from your one and only polarputt

18. My life

Once I was happy
once I was smiling
once my eyes glittered brightly
just like the sun is shining
what happened to my world,
why my happiness fly away like a bird?
why do I stay silent while everyone is talking
Why do I suddenly stop during walking
what changed my life?
why do words cut deeper than a knife?
Why do I cry at night?
Why did my life turn out to be like torn kites?
Where is my life's bright light
Why I want to jump from a height
With everyone, I am so tired of debating
There's plenty of air to breathe in but why am I still suffocating?

19. What if I fall in love?

I am not scared to love
I am scared to fall in love
what if I am a glass
which falls and scatters into a million pieces
what if I am that leave which falls
with the first drop of rain
what if I am an old house
which can no longer stand
with all the scars in it
what if I broke in a way
that can never be repaired again
at this point, I don't know whether to think with
my heart or my brain
I guess that's why I write so much about love
to understand it
I guess I am going to take my chances with you
because something inside me that our love will remain
until the universe is ended

20. When I die

When I die turn me into dust
leave a little piece of me in California
from the hands of someone I love
leave me in the bay with the shore to hug
leave me in India
at my favourite place
where I can listen to my family sing
leave me at a place with a beautiful sunset
which reminds me how beautiful life is
leave me in London but
do it without any pain
leave me under the starry night
where we love to lay down and talk
leave me at the library
where I found myself for the first time
I would say to leave me at my home
but I know a part of me will always remain there
no matter if I am not
physical here with you
but I will always be alive
in our memories and
in you

Thank you readers for choosing to read this book. I hope you like it

Printed by Libri Plureos GmbH in Hamburg, Germany